Bunny and Bee's Noisy Night

Sam Williams

ORCHARD BOOKS

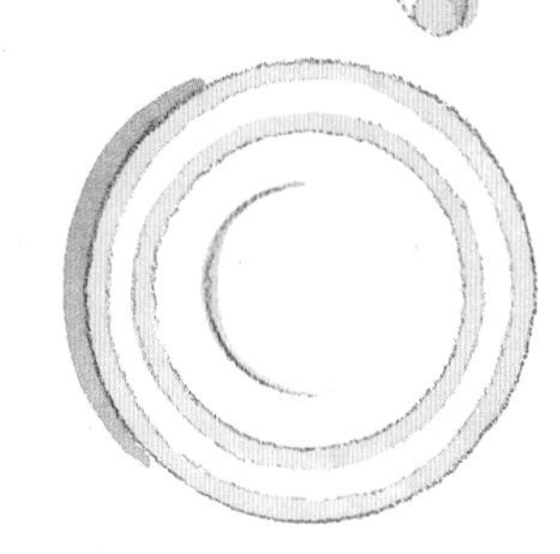

For Mussy and Bean

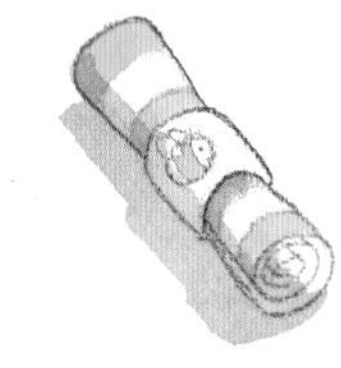

Also available:

Bunny and Bee's Playful Day

Bunny and Bee's Forest Friends

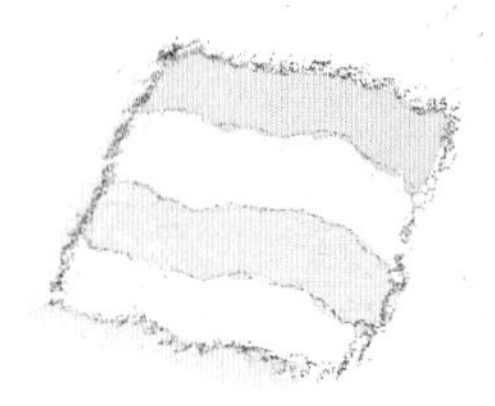

ORCHARD BOOKS
96 Leonard Street, London EC2A 4XD
Orchard Books Australia
32/45-51 Huntley Street, Alexandria, NSW 2015
ISBN 1 84121 828 6 (hardback)
ISBN 1 84362 286 6 (paperback)
First published in Great Britain in 2003
First paperback publication in 2004

A CIP catalogue record for this book is available from the British Library.
(hardback) 10 9 8 7 6 5 4 3 2 1
(paperback) 10 9 8 7 6 5 4 3 2 1
Printed in Singapore

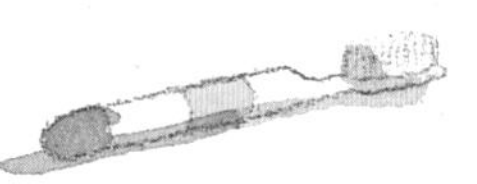

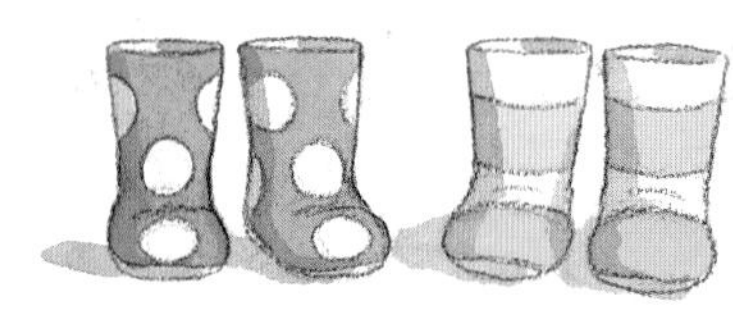

Here is a house.
A house in a tree.

The house is the home
of Bunny and Bee.

Bunny Bee

Each night before
they rest their heads,

they hug goodnight...

and climb into their beds.

The night is quiet - shhh!
Not a sound to be heard.
Not an owl, fox or badger,
Nor a cat or a bird…

but then,

“Hoot, hoot!”

hoots Owl,

to Bunny and Bee.

"Goodnight Owl," calls Bunny.
"Goodnight Owl," calls Bee.

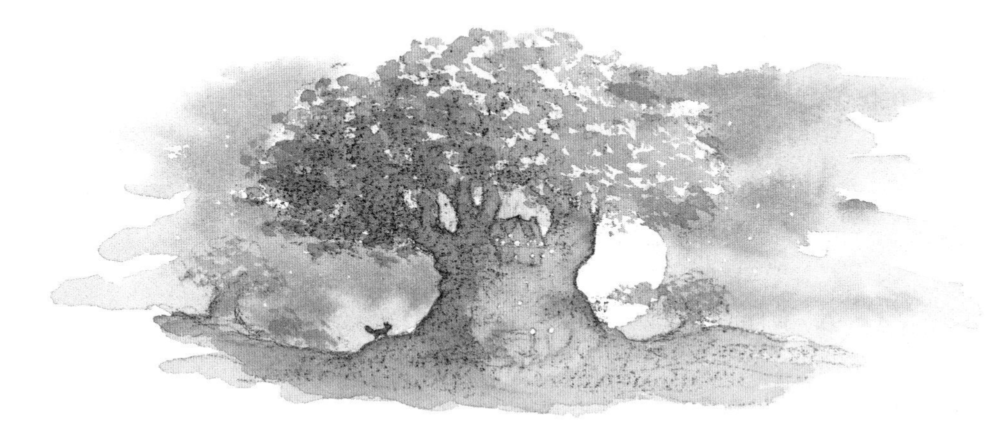

“Bark, bark!”

barks Fox, to

Bunny and Bee.

"Goodnight Fox,"
they call back,
sleepily.

“Snort, snort!”
snorts Badger,
to Bunny and Bee.

“Shhh, Badger,” says Bunny.
“Goodnight Badger,” says Bee.

“Mee-ow!”

mee-ows Cat,
to Bunny and Bee.

"Goodnight Cat!" says Bunny.
"Time for sleep!" says Bee.

It is quiet again.
Not a sound nearby.

The moon drifts lazily
across the sky.

"Tweet, tweet!"

sing the birds, as the sun starts to rise.

Poor Bunny and Bee have
such tired little eyes.

"I'm sooooo sleepy," yawns Owl.
"Me too," yawns Fox.
"Me too," yawns Badger.

“Me too,” yawns Cat.
“Me too,” yawns Bunny.
“Me too,” yawns Bee.

Shhh! Now they're all asleep
by the house in the tree.